A Note to Parents and Teachers

DK READERS is a compelling reading program for beginning readers, designed in conjunction with leading literacy experts.

Beautiful illustrations and superb full-color photographs combine with engaging, easy-to-read stories to offer a fresh approach to each subject in the series. Each DK READER is guaranteed to capture a reader's interest while developing his or her reading skills, general knowledge, and love of reading.

The five levels of DK READERS are aimed at different reading abilities, enabling you to choose the books th[illegible]re exactly right for your child:

Pre-level 1—Learning to read
Level 1—Beginning to read
Level 2—Beginning to read alone
Level 3—Reading alone
Level 4—Proficient readers

The "normal" age at which a child begins to read can be anywhere fro[illegible] three to eight years old, so these levels are only a general guideline.

No matter which level you select, you can be sure that you are helping your child learn to read, then read to learn!

LONDON, NEW YORK, MUNICH,
MELBOURNE, AND DELHI

Created by Tall Tree Ltd.
For DK
Editor Laura Gilbert
Production Alison Lenane
DTP/Designer Dean Scholey
Picture Research Hayley Smith
Picture Library Kate Ledwith

First American Edition, 2005
Published in the United States by
DK Publishing, Inc.
375 Hudson Street
New York, New York 10014

07 08 10 9 8 7 6

Library of Congress Cataloging-in-Publication Data

Donkin, Andrew.
Transformers Energon : Megatron Returns / written by Andrew Donkin.-- 1st American ed.
p. cm. -- (Dk readers)
Summary: Alpha-Quintesson hopes that by bringing Megatron back to life, he will have an ally in his effort to reawaken the evil Unicron, but Megatron has plans of his own and will let nothing stand in his way.
ISBN 978-0-7566-1152-1 (pb) -- ISBN 978-0-7566-1151-4 (hb)
[1. Science fiction.] I. Title: Megatron returns. II. Title. III. Dorling Kindersley readers.
PZ7.D7175Ttu 2005
[Fic]--dc22
2004022224

Color reproduction by Media Development and Printing Ltd., UK
Printed and bound in China by L. Rex Printing Co., Ltd.

The publisher would like to thank the following for their kind permission to reproduce their photographs:
Abbreviations key:
a-above, b-below, c-centre, r-right, l-left.
DK Images: American Museum of Natural History 28bl; Board of Trustees of the Royal Armouries 32bl; Imperial War Museum, London 22tl; Courtesy of Ministry of Defence, Pattern Room, Nottingham 23tr; NASA 36tl, 38bl, 41tr, 42cl, 46cl; Stephen Oliver 18cl.
All other images © Dorling Kindersley.
For further information see: www.dkimages.com

Discover more at
www.dk.com

Contents

MEGATRON RETURNS

Written by Andrew Donkin

Robots rule

Transformers are a race of living robots from the planet Cybertron. They have the incredible ability to transform themselves from their robot form into the shape of a vehicle, such as a car, ship, or jet aircraft.

Several million years ago, the Transformers split into two groups. These were the good Autobots, led by Optimus Prime, and the evil, war-mongering Decepticons, led by Megatron. Cybertron was soon engulfed in a terrible war.

Cybertron
Now rebuilt after the terrible civil wars and the destruction of the Unicron Battles, planet Cybertron is made from living metal.

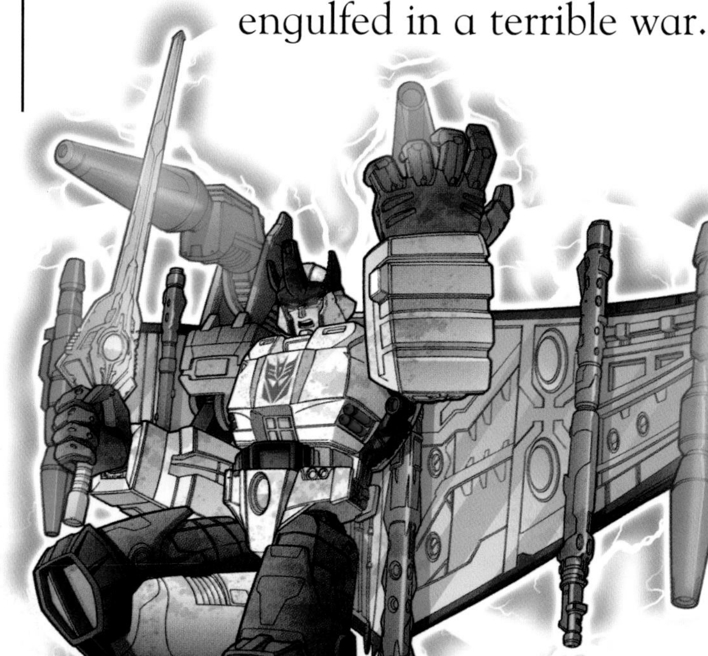

Megatron
Armed with his Primary Pulse Cannon, Megatron is the mightiest Decepticon and combines brains, strength, and cunning.

The war was brought to an end when the two opposing groups were faced by the evil of Unicron. Unicron was a planet-sized robot who was nearly as old as the universe itself. During the civil war, he fed on the hatred generated by the Transformers as they fought one another.

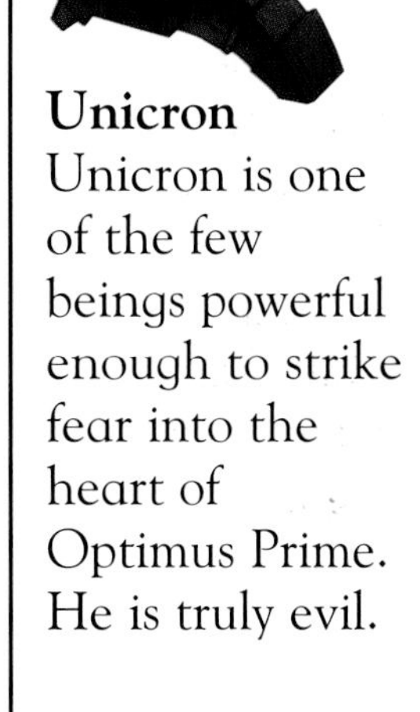

Unicron
Unicron is one of the few beings powerful enough to strike fear into the heart of Optimus Prime. He is truly evil.

Optimus Prime and Megatron realized that the only way to save their planet was to combine their forces and they became uneasy allies. Unicron was defeated but only at great cost, with Megatron sacrificing himself in the final battle.

Optimus Prime and Megatron have fought many battles across the universe.

Terrorcon attack!

For ten years after the defeat of Unicron, the galaxy has been at peace. Megatron's old gang of Decepticons now work alongside Optimus Prime and his Autobots instead of fighting them.

Transformers and humans also work together, exploring space. One of the most important concerns for both species is finding and harvesting Energon, a pure and clean energy source found deep under the surface of planets.

Sadly, this period of galactic peace was not to last.

Divebomb
Hundreds of Divebomb Terrorcons were unleashed from the interior of Unicron to do his bidding.

Hawk mode
When in hawk mode, Divebomb Terrorcons use their aerial bird-of-prey powers to devastating effect, attacking from the air.

Ocean City comes under fire from a swarm of Terrorcons and Kicker finds himself threatened by a snarling Battle Ravage.

Terrorcons
Divebomb and Battle Ravage are two types of Terrorcon. Divebomb swoops to attack in hawk mode, while Battle Ravage operates mainly in cougar mode.

Without warning, mining bases all over Mars and on Earth were attacked by a swarm of evil Transformers called Terrorcons who were out to steal Energon. The Terrorcons wanted the Energon for one unspeakable purpose—to bring the dreaded Unicron back to life!

In cougar mode, Battle Ravage Terrorcons have a mace tail that can be a powerful weapon on the battlefield.

Optimus
Optimus Prime travels between planets using a "space bridge." This allows the Transformers to cross the vast distances of space. In vehicle mode, Optimus is a huge truck and trailer.

The good guys

The leader of the Transformers is the mighty Optimus Prime. Optimus is a fierce and brave warrior. He believes that all living things have a right to freedom. Optimus Prime heads an elite team of Autobots. This team is made up of Hot Shot, Inferno, Jetfire, and the rookie Ironhide.

Hot Shot is Optimus Prime's second-in-command. He is a young Autobot who tranforms into a sports car.

Hot Shot is a vital member of Optimus Prime's elite squad.

The new member of the team is Ironhide. This rookie's first mission was to come to Earth to face the menace of the mysterious Terrorcons. An energetic warrior, his many impressive displays in battle earned him a place on the team. He transforms into a truck with a powerful cannon.

Kicker is the Autobots' human friend. He is a motorcycle-riding teenager with a stubborn streak and a big mouth. At first, Kicker didn't like taking orders from the Autobots, but he quickly learned to respect them.

Hot Shot in sports-car mode races through Ocean City.

Babysitting
Ironhide has been given the job of looking after Kicker. Neither of them wanted to work as a team, but they are learning to respect each other.

Forces of darkness

The Transformers and their human allies face a terrifying combination of foes.

Alpha-Quintesson is a strange robotic alien with four heads and four completely different personalities. He is in charge of the swarms of Terrorcons that have been attacking Earth and stealing Energon.

Realizing that he needed someone to command the Terrorcons in battle, Alpha-Quintesson brought Scorponok to life. He also recruited the former Decepticons Tidal Wave and Cyclonus.

Scorponok
Scorponok wants to be Unicron's right-hand man and lead the reformed Decepticons. It remains to be seen whether Scorponok will get his way, or whether the evil Megatron will return to stop him.

Lurking in the remains of Unicron is Alpha-Quintesson. He may not be physically strong, but he is extremely clever, evil, and cunning.

At the end of the Unicron Battles, the once-mighty Unicron was all but destroyed and his shattered remains were cast adrift in space. Unicron, however, is planning his return and each bit of stolen Energon makes him stronger.

Deep in Unicron's core is the body of Megatron, the former leader of the Decepticons. Alpha-Quintesson has dreams of bringing Megatron back to life to serve Unicron. But would Megatron ever be a willing servant for anyone?

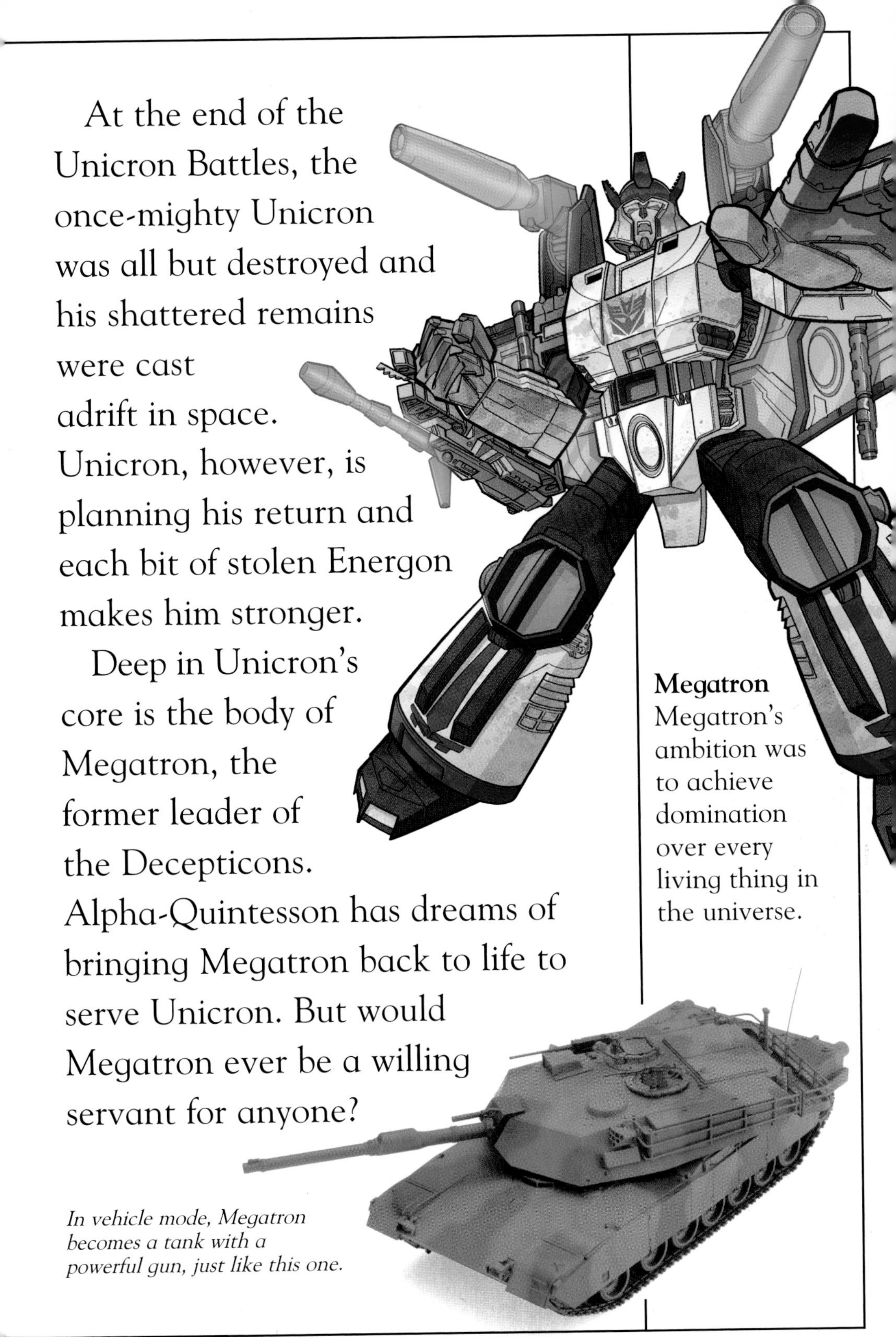

Megatron
Megatron's ambition was to achieve domination over every living thing in the universe.

In vehicle mode, Megatron becomes a tank with a powerful gun, just like this one.

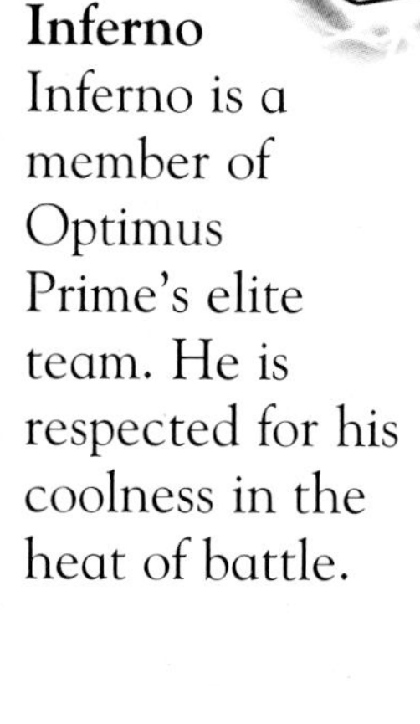

Inferno
Inferno is a member of Optimus Prime's elite team. He is respected for his coolness in the heat of battle.

Megatron lives!

The Autobot known as Inferno looked out over the mountain valley. For the past few months, everyone under Optimus Prime's command had been on edge because their bases had been raided regularly by Terrorcons. These slaves of Unicron would swoop down from nowhere to steal as much Energon as they could.

Inferno's job was to be the first line of defense against the Terrorcons. He was stationed in Blizzard City and had just heard that they were about to be attacked.

Building defenses
Earth now has gun batteries positioned near all its major Energon mines.

But this time they were ready for them.

As the Terrorcons flew down from the clear blue sky, two dozen gun batteries emerged from beneath the snow.

"Open fire! Now!" said Inferno.

A barrage of red lasers was fired by the gun batteries, blasting every Terrorcon out of the sky.

Inferno smiled. Laser batteries on the Moon had also been successful in stopping a Terrorcon attack. With all of these weapons now in place, more and more Terrorcon missions were ending in failure.

Space guns
Powerful gun batteries are also used to protect important Energon mines on the Moon, Mars, and in the Asteroid Belt.

Like the Transformers' cannons, guns have been used to defend cities and castles for hundreds of years. Cannons were invented in the 14th century by a monk named Berthold Schwarz.

Leadership
Tidal Wave and Cyclonus stand in front of the damaged body of Megatron. Many of the Decepticons long to have Megatron return to lead them once more. They feel directionless without him in control.

Deep within a cloud of dark cosmic matter, the remains of the once-great Unicron drifted through space. Inside, Alpha-Quintesson was not happy. It was his job to gather enough Energon for Unicron.

"They seem to have improved their defensive capabilities," said Alpha-Quintesson with a snarl. "How dare they get in our way."

With so little Energon now left, Alpha-Quintesson could sense exactly where every last power unit was going.

"There shouldn't be a power drain in that chamber unless... oh no!"

Cyclonus is the most reckless Decepticon. In vehicle mode, he becomes a helicopter armed with proton rockets.

In the chamber in question, Tidal Wave and Cyclonus, both former Decepticons who had returned to bad ways, were standing looking at the remains of their former leader, the once mighty Megatron. Megatron's body hung embedded in the chamber wall, as if the hideous twisted structure had grown around him.

"Our deepest apologies that we failed to get any Energon to awaken you, sir, but we were ambushed," said Tidal Wave, sadly.

Tidal Wave remains devoted to his former leader.

Trapped in Unicron

It was long believed that Megatron had been utterly destroyed in the final Unicron Battles. However, with the remains of his body embedded deep inside Unicron, was it possible that he had survived?

"It seems that someone in here has been stealing our Energon!" said Scorponok, entering the chamber. Tidal Wave and Cyclonus shrank away from Scorponok's furious gaze.

"Alpha-Quintesson has just discovered that Megatron has been secretly taking Energon from Unicron for months. I am here to terminate Megatron for good."

The chamber shook with a sound like distant thunder. Megatron's crumpled form began to glow with a brilliant white light.

"Megatron lives!" gasped Tidal Wave, astonished.

The blaze of light engulfed the chamber. When it faded, Megatron stood before them, reborn in a powerful new form.

Megatron's old body seems lifeless, but appearances can be deceptive.

Talking heads
Alpha-Quintesson has four heads, each with its own personality.

Megatron has managed to build himself a new, more powerful body, using the Energon that he has been secretly stealing.

"I am back!"

It was a sight that Tidal Wave and Cyclonus never thought they would see again.

"Scorponok, you have tried to steal my leadership of the Decepticons. You'll pay for that!" hissed Megatron.

"You don't scare me!" snarled Scorponok. He ordered dozens of Terrorcons to attack Megatron. However, Megatron simply smashed them aside with his amazing brute strength.

Tail stinger
Living up to his name, Scorponok can transform himself into scorpion mode, complete with an Energon stinger.

The battle between Scorponok and Megatron can have only one winner.

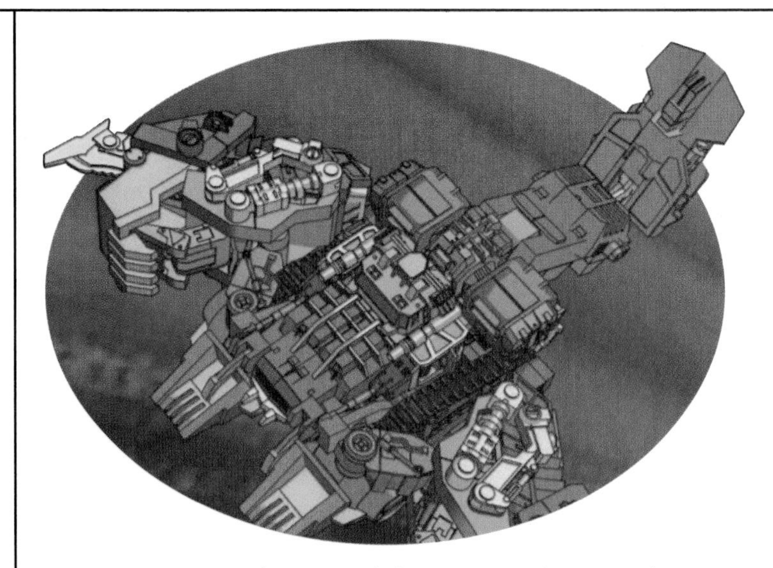

Boxing
Scorponok and Megatron engage in hand-to-hand combat. Boxing is one of the oldest forms of hand-to-hand combat in the world. Its history dates back to the ancient Greeks, who included it in their Olympic Games.

Scorponok quickly transformed into scorpion mode and leaped at Megatron. The ancient warrior grabbed Scorponok by the throat and threw him across the chamber.

"I have never felt more alive!" exclaimed Megatron.

Megatron landed blow after blow on Scorponok.

"I give in, Megatron! You win!" pleaded Scorponok.

Megatron reached down and put his hand over Scorponok's forehead. Using three million volts of electricity, he branded Scorponok with the badge of the Decepticons.

Scorponok screamed and lay defeated at Megatron's feet.

"It wasn't my plan to terminate you. It was all Alpha-Quintesson's idea," said Scorponok, weakly.

Megatron headed straight for Alpha-Quintesson's lair, only to discover that the strange creature had fled in terror. Alpha-Quintesson knew that he could not fight Megatron on his own. Perhaps bringing Megatron back to life hadn't been a good idea, thought Alpha-Quintesson as he made his escape through the remains of Unicron.

Karate
Another form of hand-to-hand combat is karate. Karate is the martial art of unarmed combat.

Megatron is back and he is stronger than ever, showing Scorponok that he is really in charge of the Decepticons and branding him with their badge.

In charge
Hot Shot is in charge of protecting the vital Energon mines located in Plains City.

Standing on the edge of Plains City, Hot Shot looked up into a sky that was dark with Terrorcons. Hot Shot had been commander of the Autobot forces on Earth until the recent conflict had brought Optimus Prime back to the planet.

A laser is a powerful beam of light. Some guns have laser sights to help the user see where the gun is being pointed.

Hot Shot pointed his laser cannon skyward and opened fire. The Energon cannons should be enough to handle this attack, he thought. Then his circuits ran cold as he spotted a sinister and familiar shape in the center of the swarm.

"It can't be..."

Realizing this was no ordinary Terrorcon attack, Optimus Prime, Inferno, Ironhide, and Kicker rushed through a space bridge from Ocean City to Plains City on a desperate rescue mission.

"Man, it must have been ugly," said Kicker, surveying the battlefield as they arrived.

Kicker would not forget what he saw next for as long as he lived.

Standing in the center of the battlefield was Megatron and he was holding the battered body of Hot Shot... who was missing his right arm!

Musical lasers
Lasers are not just used in weapons. A CD player has a laser inside it. There are tiny pits on the surface of a CD and these are read by the laser which translates them into music.

Hot Shot has taken a battering from the newly returned Megatron and is now unconscious.

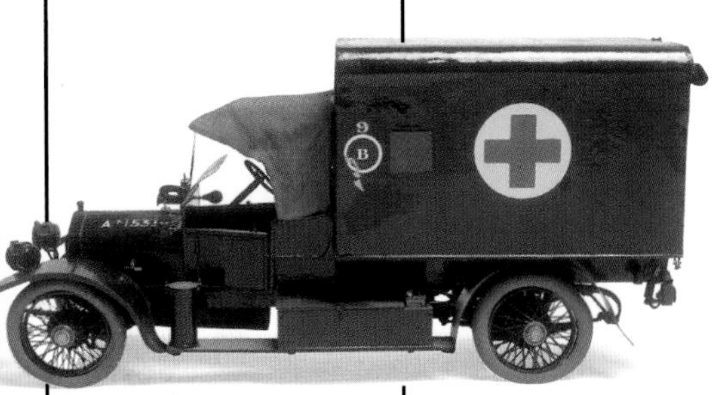

First aid
The Red Cross is an organization that was created to care for wounded soldiers on the battlefield.

Megatron's raid

The Autobots and Kicker were upset at the sight of the injured Hot Shot.

"I'm guessing you're surprised to see me?" said Megatron with a wicked smile.

"Hot Shot!" cried Ironhide.

"It's just like old times, isn't it?" said Megatron, casually throwing Hot Shot to the ground.

"You monster!" shouted Kicker.

The Autobot team and the Decepticons faced each other. Neither side was ready to make the first move.

The Autobots can survive many injuries, but some severe ones threaten even their lives.

"I know what you want, Megatron," said Optimus. "You want our Energon and then you're going after Unicron, aren't you?"

"If I bring him back to life, I'll make him serve me!" said Megatron. "And the universe will be mine."

"But that'll never happen, because we're going to stop you! Right, Optimus?" said Kicker.

Megatron raised a long glowing sword, ready for action.

"Well Prime, are you going to try and stop me? As you can see, I still have the Star Saber."

Rapid fire
Transformers are equipped with cannons that fire powerful laser blasts. Modern human weapons, such as this semiautomatic rifle, can fire several bullets every second.

The good guys and the bad guys face off, while behind them more Terrorcon reinforcements fill the sky.

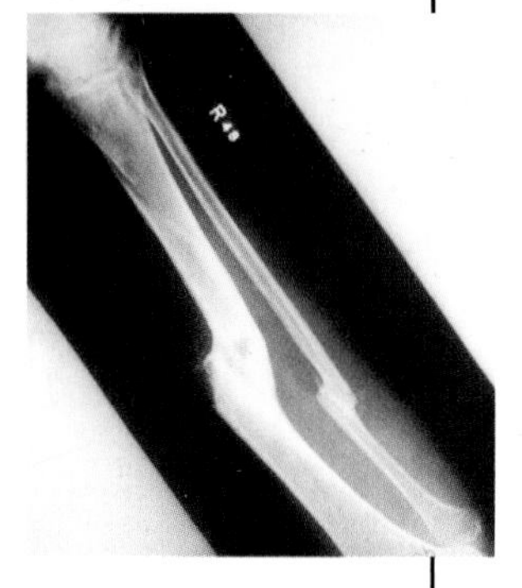

Healing injuries
While liquid Energon can heal Autobots, human doctors use other methods to heal people. X-rays allow doctors to see inside the human body.

Optimus Prime raised his hand to stop Kicker and the Autobots.

"We're going to withdraw," announced Optimus.

"But we've got to do something!" shouted Kicker.

"Hot Shot's well-being takes priority over everything else. We must withdraw back to Ocean City."

Back in Ocean City, Hot Shot was rushed to the medical center and placed in a tank of liquid Energon. In small doses, liquid Energon would heal his wounds and restore his damaged armor.

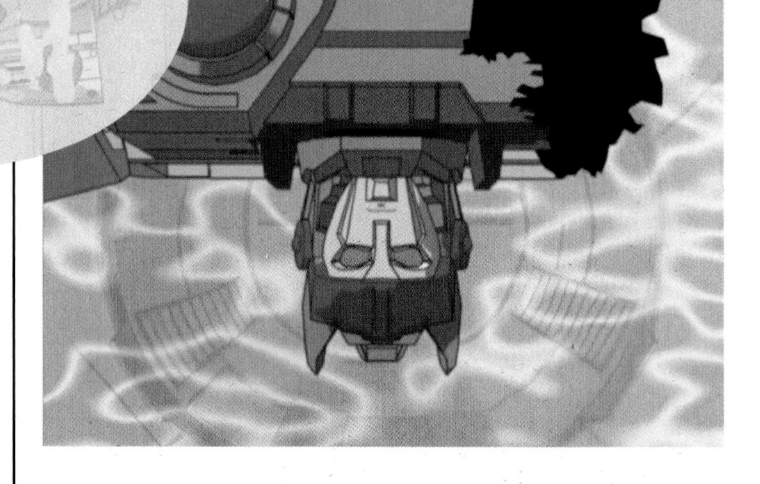

As soon as Hot Shot is placed into the healing tank, the liquid Energon gets to work, repairing the Autobot's body piece by piece.

"I really hope Hot Shot is going to be okay in there," said Ironhide.

"He will. I'll see to it," Inferno assured him.

Optimus Prime gathered a group of Omnicons around him in the center of their lab. These Transformers were designed to do scientific work, rather than fight like Optimus and his team.

"During the confrontation with the Decepticons, I took a scan of Megatron's sword. I want you to create some cloned copies of it. We're going to need them."

"Okay, boss, we're on it," said one of the Omnicons.

Concern
Hot Shot's fellow Autobots all watch his progress with concern, especially Inferno, Hot Shot's combination partner.

To help a broken bone heal properly, the limb is usually put in a cast to protect it and to stop any unwanted movement.

Loyal warrior
Of all the Decepticons, Demolisher was the one most loyal to Megatron, obeying his orders without question.

The next day, Optimus Prime stood in the control room of Ocean City. He was expecting trouble.

Optimus guessed that Megatron would have already delivered the Energon he stole the day before to Unicron. Optimus knew that Megatron's plan to revive Unicron and control him would be disastrous for everyone. No one could control a force as powerful as Unicron.

Blackbird
Although not as quick as Jetfire, the Blackbird was one of the fastest jet aircraft ever built. It was first flown in the early 1960s by the American military and could reach speeds of up to 2,100 miles per hour (3,360 kilometers per hour).

At fast speeds, the metal exterior of the Blackbird reached 400°F (204°C).

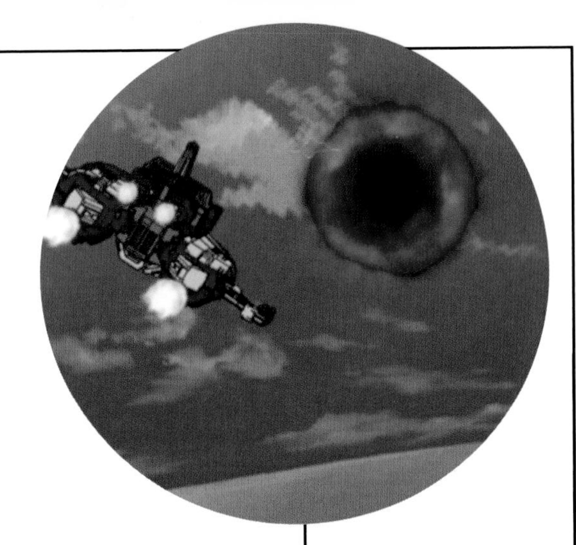

"Commander, what about Demolisher?" said Jetfire. "He's still on guard duty at the outer gate. Should we relieve him? He is a Decepticon."

"He *was* a Decepticon," said Optimus. "He's not anymore."

Suddenly, alarms sounded on the central console, signaling a new Terrorcon attack.

"There's a space bridge opening about 19 miles south of the city," said Inferno from the control room.

"There's no Energon out there!" said Kicker, puzzled.

"Maybe it's a trap," agreed Optimus. "Jetfire, fly out there and take a look."

Jetfire immediately transformed into shuttle mode and blasted off from Ocean City, heading straight toward the danger area.

Jetfire quickly closes in on the space bridge opening over the ocean.

Jumbo jet
The Boeing 747, known as a jumbo jet, has four jet engines and can reach a speed of 550 miles per hour (880 kilometers per hour).

Demolisher stands in the pouring rain, guarding the entry gates to Ocean City.

"There's nothing here, Optimus," reported Jetfire when he reached the space bridge. Violet lightning suddenly crackled through the rain clouds as a space bridge opened above Ocean City.

"Sir, there's another space bridge opening up less than one mile to the north of the city!"

The first space bridge was just a diversion to lure the Autobots away.

"This is it. Get ready, men!" ordered Optimus Prime.

Outside in the pouring rain, Demolisher was standing guard at the outer gate. Looking up into the sky he found himself face to face with his former leader—Megatron.

Blue whale
The waters below Ocean City are home to some of the biggest creatures ever to have lived. The largest is the blue whale, which can be 100 feet (30 meters) long.

"So it's true then. You really are alive," stammered Demolisher.

"Now Demolisher, I want you to prove your loyalty to me by opening up this fortress," demanded Megatron.

Demolisher was suddenly torn between loyalty to his new Autobot friends and loyalty to his old wartime leader. Eventually, there could only be one winner.

"I'm yours, Megatron!" said Demolisher, blasting open the gates of Ocean City.

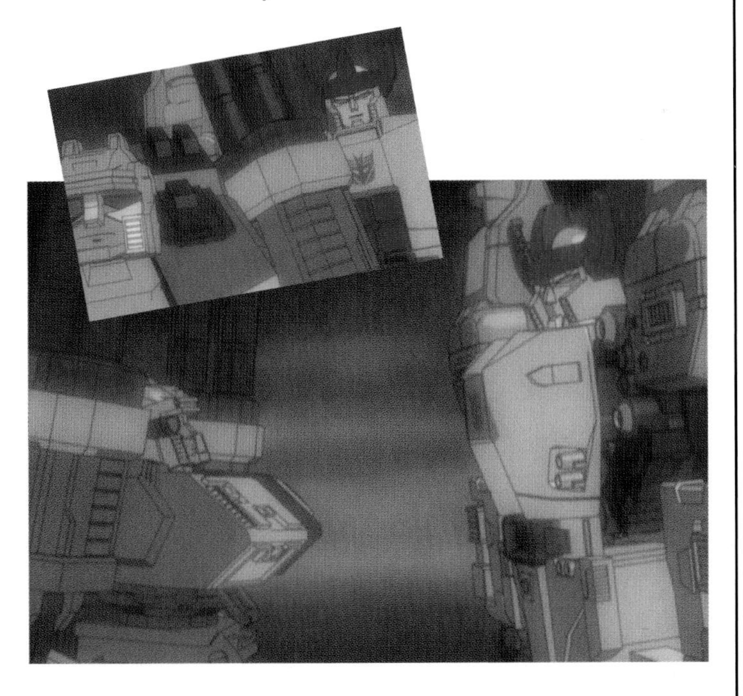

Diving
Ocean City is surrounded by water. When humans want to explore beneath the waves, they need to use specialized diving equipment.

Demolisher finds himself caught in the middle as his old leader Megatron returns and asks him to betray his new friends Kicker and Optimus Prime.

The Terrorcons make for Ocean City's lab, where the Energon is stored.

DNA
Just as the Omnicons cloned the sword, scientists can clone plants and animals by copying their DNA (deoxyribonucleic acid).

DNA is a chainlike chemical that is found in every living cell. DNA contains all the information about a living thing and it passes this information from generation to generation.

With the gates open, a pack of Battle Ravage Terrorcons in cougar mode ran inside Ocean City to hunt for Energon. They raced down the streets of the city ripping apart anything that got in their way.

"All right. We're going to take all the Energon they have and destroy this city!" gloated Megatron, as he watched his forces at work.

"Not so fast," demanded Optimus Prime, blocking Megatron's path.

Inside the city, Kicker ran panting into the Omnicons' lab.

"Is the clone of Megatron's sword ready?" he shouted.

"Here you go. Catch!" called one of the Omnicons, throwing the massive blade at Kicker. Kicker grabbed it and ran out of the lab into the corridor, only to see a pack of charging Terrorcons heading for him.

He raised the huge sword and charged the Terrorcons, slicing them in two. But he had no time to stay and fight. He had to get the sword to Optimus—and fast.

Molten Energon
The skilled Omnicons use molten Energon at high temperatures as the raw material for the cloned swords.

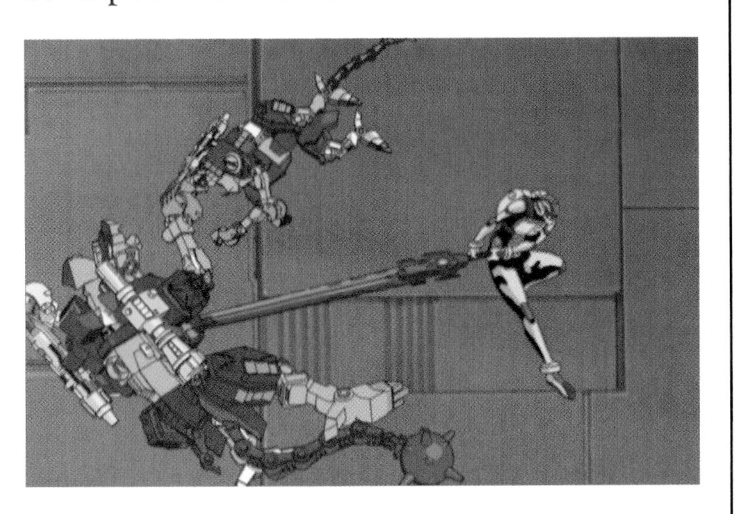

Kicker uses the massive sword to slice his way through the enemy ranks.

Star Saber
Megatron's sword is the Star Saber. It is made up of three Mini-Cons that can join together.

Outside, the battle was not going well for Optimus Prime. He was spending most of his efforts simply avoiding Megatron's deadly sword.

"This time my blade won't miss!" said Megatron.

Suddenly Kicker ran into view.

"Optimus! Here you go!" he shouted, throwing the cloned Star Saber to Optimus.

Megatron was furious. "That's my sword! How did you make a copy of it?" he demanded.

Swords have been valued as weapons all over the world. Each culture has its own distinct style, such as these Japanese samurai swords.

"It's just something our friends, the Omnicons, came up with. And it's every bit as powerful as your sword," said Optimus.

"We'll see about that, Prime!"

The two old foes moved forward and their weapons smashed together with incredible force, shaking Ocean City to its very foundations. Optimus and Megatron blasted through the sky. Their swords flashed with lightning fast movements.

"You'll never beat me, Optimus Prime!" said Megatron, arrogantly.

On guard
Fencing is a sport where two people duel with lightweight, flexible swords.

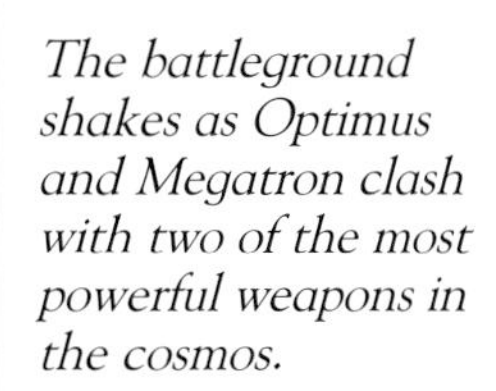

The battleground shakes as Optimus and Megatron clash with two of the most powerful weapons in the cosmos.

Megatron reborn
Megatron's new body, with its triple-changing capabilities, is even more powerful than his last one.

"Megatron, look!" cried the Decepticon Cyclonus.

Inferno, Jetfire, Ironhide, and Kicker were all running toward the battlefield and each of them was carrying a clone of Megatron's sword. It was a disaster for the Decepticon leader!

"This time we've got them right where we want them," said Kicker.

Megatron looked around and weighed up the odds.

"I still have one trick up my sleeve," he promised, as a space bridge began to open above him. The Decepticon leader had decided to retreat.

The battle turns against Megatron as Ironhide and Hot Shot join the battle, each holding a clone of Megatron's sword.

"Come with us, Demolisher," ordered Megatron.

"Don't go with him, Demolisher," pleaded Ironhide. "It doesn't have to be like this."

But it was no use. Megatron and his Decepticons disappeared through the whirling purple hole of the space bridge above their heads.

"They got away!" said Kicker, with disappointment in his voice.

"It's too bad that Demolisher decided to go with them," said Optimus, sadly. "I had hoped that we could show him that there was a better way than war."

Energon power
To create a space bridge for their escape Megatron uses a piece of specially prepared Energon.

Now that the odds have turned against them, Megatron and his Decepticons make a hasty retreat through a space bridge.

Asteroid battle

For the next few weeks, Optimus and his men kept a careful watch for any signs of renewed Terrorcon activity. Megatron and their other enemies were obviously planning and biding their time.

The tension was broken by an emergency call from Carlos Lopez in Midway Gate Station 08.

"Optimus, I've just picked up an unidentified spacecraft on radar. It's moving toward the Energon mines in the Asteroid Belt!" reported Carlos.

Hot stuff
The Asteroid Belt is part of the solar system, at the center of which is the Sun. Temperatures inside the Sun can reach a scorching 29 million °F (16 million °C).

The Autobots have many Energon mining bases in the solar system. This one is in orbit above the surface of Mars.

"Even more worrying, we've just lost radio contact with the mines completely. Someone must be blocking our radio signal."

"That means they must have established a base in the Asteroid Belt. We must protect our valuable Energon mines up there. Our objective is clear. We must set up a new battlefront in the Asteroid Belt and stop the Decepticons at all costs. So let's move it!" ordered the Autobot leader.

Optimus Prime and his elite team of Autobots raced for the space bridge.

Carlos on Mars
The Autobot space station above Mars is run by Optimus Prime's old human friend Carlos.

Comets also form part of the solar system. Perhaps the most famous comet is Halley's Comet, a lump of rock and ice that passes the Earth every 76 years.

Optimus Prime and the other Autobots arrive in the Asteroid Belt on the hunt for Megatron and the Decepticons. However, Kicker is feeling uneasy about being in this region of space.

As they emerged from the space bridge, Kicker remembered why he hated asteroid fields so much. His head seemed to spin and his stomach flipped over. His mind flashed back to when he had been cast adrift in an asteroid field when he was just a little kid. It was his worst nightmare.

"So Kicker, do you sense anything? Which one of the Energon mines is Megatron at right now?" asked Optimus, looking out at the asteroid field. It went on for as far as his sensors could see.

Space rock
Asteroids are large lumps of space rock. They can measure a few feet or many miles across.

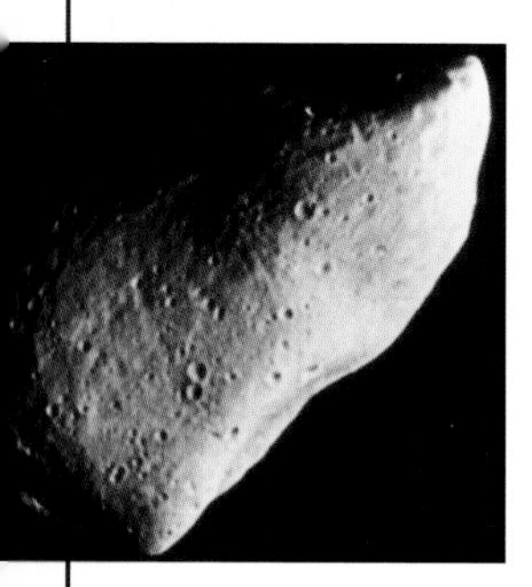

Traveling through the asteroid field, Kicker remembers when he was lost in space as a child.

"I don't know. My ESP is not that accurate, especially in this asteroid field. But I get a sense we should head in this direction," said Kicker, pointing out into space and hoping that it was the right way.

"If we have to search all of these asteroids, it's going to take all day," said Inferno, gazing at the thousands of pieces of rock floating about him.

"I should be able to pinpoint their position more accurately when we get moving," said Kicker, hopefully.

Asteroid Belt
Asteroids orbit our Sun. Most of them occur in a belt between the orbits of Mars and Jupiter.

Overrun
The enemy Terrorcon forces have one big advantage—there are hundreds of them.

Megatron and his Decepticons left a trail of ransacked Energon mines in their wake as they cut a path through the Asteroid Belt. The Terrorcons were able to steal plenty of Energon. Demolisher then reminded his leader that there was still lots of Energon left in Lunar City. The Decepticons made that their next target.

The Omnicons working in Lunar City fled in terror, leaving more Energon for Megatron and his evil band to steal.

Lunar City's laser cannon batteries blast at the Terrorcons as they swoop from the sky to steal the Energon.

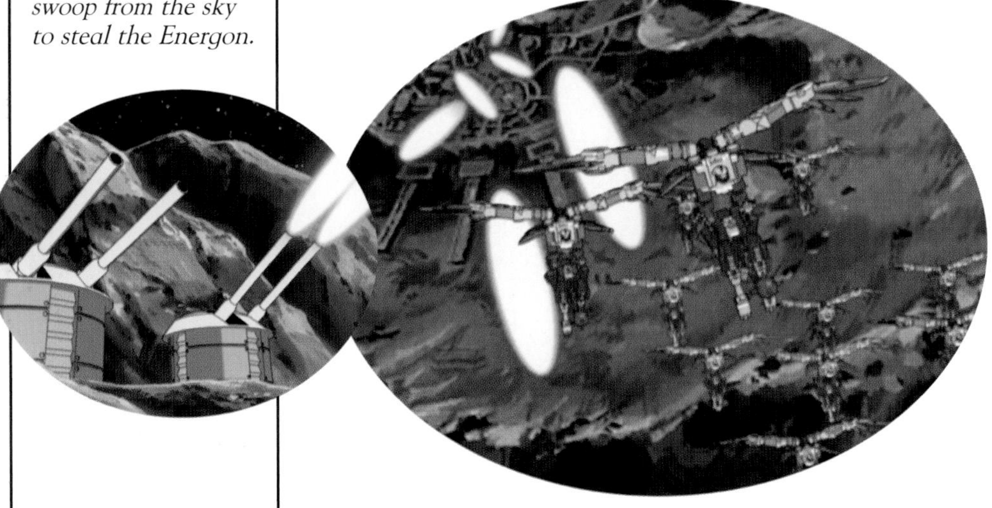

“There!” said Kicker. “Look over there. I’m getting a strange feeling that’s what we’re looking for. That asteroid looks alive... like part of...”

Craters
The craters on the Moon have been caused by impacts from space over millions of years.

“Unicron!” blurted out Hot Shot. “Unicron’s body must have broken up and pieces of it are hidden out here in the Asteroid Belt. We’ve got to destroy him!”

The Autobots opened fired on the strange-looking asteroid. However, even the strongest energy blasts from their laser cannons did not leave a mark on it.

Recognizing the remains of Unicron, the Autobots open fire in an effort to destroy him once and for all.

Kicker watches the Autobots depart, leaving him alone.

Flying free
NASA has developed a backpack that lets astronauts fly free and untied while out in space.

The asteroid suddenly began to move away as if in reaction to the attack.

"We need to follow. It's too dangerous for you, Kicker, so you stay here," said Optimus as the Autobots blasted off, leaving Kicker floating in space.

"Oh man," said Kicker to himself. He began to remember being lost and floating helplessly in space when he was a child.

Suddenly, there was a huge explosion right next to Hot Shot. In the distance, Scorponok was standing on the surface of another asteroid firing Energon-charged laser blasts at the Autobots.

Jetfire was down and he needed rescuing fast. Optimus transformed to Optimus Super Mode and swooped down, smashing Scorponok to the ground.

It looked like things were finally turning Optimus Prime's way when he heard a familiar, but unwelcome, voice behind him.

"Hello, Optimus!"

It was Megatron, and with him were the Decepticons and a huge army of Terrorcons that had surrounded the Autobots.

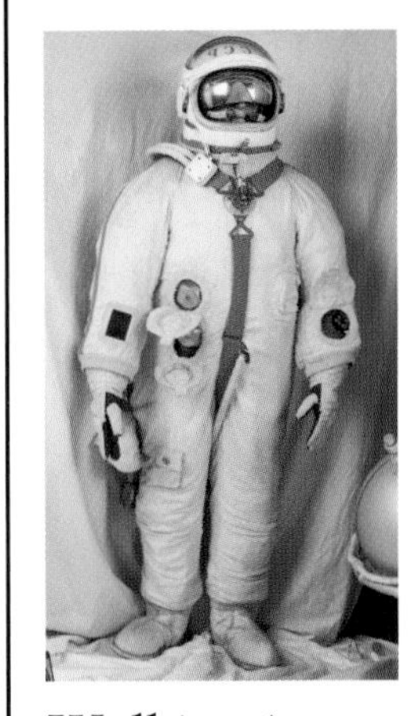

Walking in space
The first human being to ever perform a space walk was the Russian cosmonaut Alexei A. Leonov in 1965.

Megatron arrives, bringing Tidal Wave and the rest of the Decepticons with him.

Optimus discovers that the asteroid under the Autobots' feet is full of Energon.

"Glad you could join us," said Hot Shot.

"If you're trying to make me angry, you're doing a good job. But trust me, junior, you wouldn't like me when I'm angry," replied Megatron.

"Optimus, we're standing right on a huge Energon deposit," said Ironhide in alarm.

"Don't fire this way, Megatron, or this whole asteroid will go up!" said Optimus.

Optimus should have known better. Saying that to Megatron was like waving a red flag in front of a bull.

Meteorite
A meteorite is a piece of space debris, possibly from an asteroid or a comet, that hits the surface of the Earth.

"And you'll have a front row seat to watch!" said Megatron, firing a blast of his laser cannon straight at the Energon.

As the laser blast hit, the entire asteroid began to shake. Megatron's blast had triggered a chain reaction! The Autobots grabbed the fallen Jetfire and, as the asteroid blew apart around them, made their escape with just microseconds to spare.

The last thing Optimus heard was the laughter of Megatron, delighting in the chaos and destruction. Megatron was certainly back.

Dinosaur doom
Many scientists think that the dinosaurs became extinct because of a climatic change brought about by a huge asteroid colliding with the Earth.

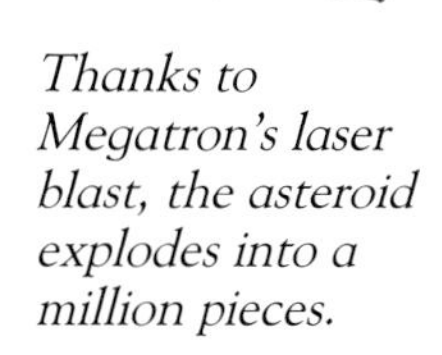

Thanks to Megatron's laser blast, the asteroid explodes into a million pieces.

Protection
Energon towers are built to protect the Earth from Megatron and the Terrorcons.

The Autobots scanned the Asteroid Belt and rescued Kicker. The stranded teenager had never been so glad to see them.

When they all returned to Ocean City, they were in for quite a shock. Things had changed. All of the civilians who had been evacuated from the city after the earliest Terrorcon attacks had now returned to their homes.

That night there was a meeting in the control center. Dr. Jones, Kicker's father, had returned from Cyberton and he explained his plans for the defense of planet Earth.

The Energon towers protect planet Earth and its atmosphere. The atmosphere is the layer of gases that surrounds the planet and keeps its temperatures moderate, thus ensuring that life can survive.

"I propose we build towers that are capable of transmitting Energon waves. When these are activated, they will form a protecting grid around the planet."

The idea was met by cheers and excited applause from the crowd.

"Do you think my dad's idea can work?" whispered Kicker.

"I'm sure it will," Optimus reassured him. "It's a great idea. It should keep Earth safe for now. But with Megatron alive again, we will never truly be able to relax."

Inner Earth
Many valuable mineral deposits are found in the solid outer crust of the Earth. Many miles beneath this crust are layers of liquid rock that make up the Earth's core.

The Energon waves affect only the Terrorcons and Decepticons and create a protecting grid around the Earth.

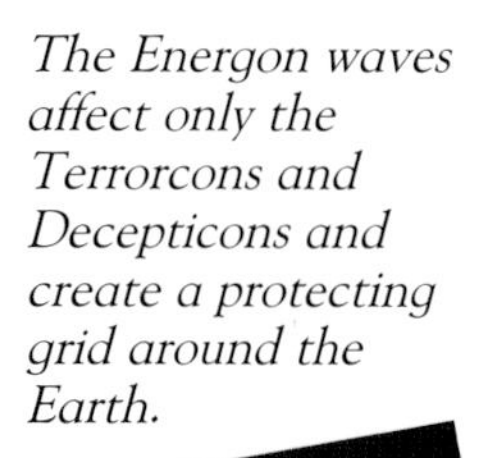

Glossary

alien
A being or creature from another planet.

allies
People who fight together on the same side during a war.

ancient
Something that is very old or from the past.

Asteroid Belt
A collection of asteroids that orbits the Sun between the planets Mars and Jupiter.

branded
To have a symbol burned into a person's or animal's skin.

cloned
To copy a person or animal using the original's DNA.

console
A control panel.

core
The center of a planet.

deposit
A natural occurrence of a mineral or rock.

diversion
An event designed to distract people from your real purpose.

embedded
To be deep within something.

engulfed
To be completely surrounded or covered.

ESP
Extrasensory perception. A person's ability to see events that occur in the future.

foundations
The base of something.

galaxy
A group of billions of stars held together by gravity.

gun batteries
A cluster or group of weapons.

hand-to-hand combat
Two individuals fighting each other.

harvest
To collect a crop or mineral when it is ready.

lab
A place where scientific work or experiments are carried out.

lasers
Very powerful beams of light.

microseconds
Each microsecond is a one-millionth part of a second.

pack
A group of animals that moves together.

pinpoint
To spot where something is located.

sacrificing
To give up something valuable for the greater good.

scan
To assess something to learn more about it.

solar system
The family of planets, asteroids, and comets that orbit the Sun.

stammer
To repeat a word without meaning to.

stubborn
To refuse to change your mind.

swarm
A group of flying things.

terminate
To end something.

universe
Everything that exists in space.

warrior
Someone whose main occupation is fighting.

withdraw
To retreat and leave.